NURSE MATILDA
GOES TO TOWN

by Christianna Brand
illustrated by Edward Ardizzone

BLOOMSBURY
CHILDREN'S
BOOKS

To Simon Taylor
my godson

Published in Great Britain in 2005 by Bloomsbury Publishing Plc
38 Soho Square, London, W1D 3HB

First published in 1967 by The Brockhampton Press Ltd

Text copyright © 1967 Christianna Brand
Illustrations copyright © 1967 Edward Ardizzone
The right of Christianna Brand to be identified as the author of this work has been
asserted by the Estate of Christianna Brand in accordance with the Copyright,
Designs and Patents Act, 1988
The right of Edward Ardizzone to be identified as the illustrator of this work has
been asserted by the Estate of Edward Ardizzone in accordance with the Copyright,
Designs and Patents Act, 1988

A CIP catalogue record of this book is available from the British Library

ISBN 0 7475 7677 7

Printed and bound in Italy by Artegrafica S. p. A. Verona

1 3 5 7 9 10 8 6 4 2

· All papers used by Bloomsbury Publishing are natural, recyclable products
made from wood grown in well-managed forests. The manufacturing processes
conform to the environmental regulations of the country of origin.

NCE upon a time there were a mother and father called Mr and Mrs Brown and they had a huge family of children; and all the children were terribly, terribly naughty.

One day Mrs Brown went up to the school-room to speak to her children and this is what they were doing:

Tora had put glue in the sandwiches.

Emma had made a large chocolate cake out of mud.

David had put a toad in the milk-jug – and Tim was under the table tying Nanny's feet to the legs of her chair with her shoe-laces. All the other children were doing simply dreadful things too.

Mrs Brown was very sweet, but she really was rather foolish about her darling children and never believed that they could possibly be naughty. So she said, 'Good afternoon, Nanny. I hope you are all enjoying your tea?'

Nanny was having a terrible time with her false teeth because of the glue in the sandwiches. She tried to say, 'Stand up, children, and say good afternoon to your dear Mama,' but it came out, 'Mmph, mmph, mmph . . .' She stood up, herself, to give a good example and fell flat down on the table because of her tied-up legs, with her face in the mud cake. At that moment the toad got tired of the milk-jug and took one huge leap out of it and landed on top of her head. Wearing him like a little mottled hat, she raised her poor, mud-clotted face to Mrs Brown, gave her one long, baleful look and, with the chair still tied to her, hopped and hobbled out of the room. Mrs Brown knew that look very well. It meant that she was going to have to go to the Agency and get another new Nanny for her darling children.

Some of *you* darling children will have read about how Nurse Matilda once came to the Brown family and made them all good and well-behaved. She was terribly ugly when she arrived, but as they got gooder and gooder, so she had become prettier and prettier, until she ended up quite lovely and all surrounded in a sort of golden glow. I'm afraid the children had slipped back very badly since then; and as if she hadn't got enough, Mrs Brown had gone out and adopted several more and they were just as naughty as their new brothers and sisters. Even she began to think that it would be a good idea if Nurse Matilda could come back and begin all over again.

Especially as . . .

Especially as the children were all going to stay with their Great-Aunt Adelaide, in town.

Most children have at least one fearsome aunt or even great-aunt. The Brown children had this truly fearsome great-aunt, Great-Aunt Adelaide Stitch.

'Now, children,' said Mrs Brown, 'I have some news for you. Your papa and I are going abroad for a holiday and you are all going to stay with Aunt Adelaide Stitch.'

The children would all have burst into most terrible exclamations of horror, but they couldn't because of the glue in the sandwiches; and Mrs Brown beamed round upon them and went happily back to the drawing-room. 'The children

are speechless with pleasure,' she said to Mr Brown. 'Oh, dear,' groaned Mr Brown, glumly. He had less faith than Mrs Brown and he thought that the children had probably already got plans for being naughty at Great-Aunt Adelaide's. Great-Aunt Adelaide was very rich and she was going to leave him all her money when she died. He didn't want her to die a bit, but when she did the money would come in very handy. He really did have so many children.

The children were by no means speechless when at last they got free of the glue. 'It's too *horr*ible!' they said. 'It'll be *awf*ul! And she lives in

London!' 'Ick *hog*gigig,' echoed the Baby. 'Ickle-ge—*or*kig! Anke livinging *Gung*-king!' It was a splendid baby and talked a language all of its own.

Great-Aunt Adelaide Stitch was a terrible old person – very gaunt and tall, with an angry little eye like the eye of a rhinoceros and a nose like the horn of a rhinoceros, turned upside-down. She lived in a big house, as tall and gaunt-looking as herself, with a neat London garden round it with green cardboard lawns and all the flowers marshalled in their beds like soldiers on parade. With her, nowadays, lived Evangeline. Evangeline had once been the poor little tweeny-maid in the Browns' home in the country. Great-Aunt Adelaide Stitch had tried to adopt one of the Brown children and somehow had managed to get Evangeline instead. Fortunately Evangeline enjoyed living with her very much, because at least it was better than being a put-upon tweeny-maid; and she now had, as promised by Aunt Adelaide at the time of her adoption:

Her own suite of rooms decorated in chocolate brown, a huge wardrobe of absolutely hideous clothes which, however, they both thought most beautiful, and –

  A pug dog

Aunt Adelaide

Evangeline

A canary
A writing-desk
A work-box
And private tuition in
elocution,
deportment,
French,
German,
Italian, and, above all, the pianoforte.

She had profited greatly from all these benefits and by now, I'm afraid, instead of being a cheerful little lump, she had become a stout little, horrid little prig. But she was just exactly what Great-Aunt Adelaide liked.

Evangeline was standing at the front door when the children arrived in a fleet of four-wheeler cabs; her pug was beside her and they were both looking forward eagerly to welcoming their guests. (The pug had a most original name: it was Pug – that was the kind of girl Evangeline was; her canary was called Canary. But still she had the example of Great-Aunt Adelaide before her. Great-Aunt Adelaide had a parrot and its name was Parrot.)

The children had brought their two

dachshunds, Sugar and Spice, and the looks on their faces when they set their bright, twinkly eyes upon Pug, made Pug's welcome a lot less eager.

There were so many children in Mr and Mrs Brown's family that we never have got round to writing down all their names; especially now, with the extra adopted ones. Even their own mother and father had to divide them into the Big Ones and the Middling Ones and the Little Ones and the Tinies. There was also the Baby and the Littlest Baby and now there was a Littler Baby Still, but the last two babies couldn't walk or talk, so they really were rather dull. The oldest baby talked a language all of its own, as we have seen. It wore a rather bundly collection of nappies which always seemed just about to fall down, but never quite did.

They all climbed out of the cabs as Evangeline stumped down the front door steps to greet them, with Pug on one side of her and Miss Prawn on the other. Miss Prawn was her governess. Summer and winter she suffered dreadfully from chilblains on her poor, thin hands.

'Oh, the pretty dears! How charming!' cried

Miss Prawn, clasping the chilblains as the children closed the doors of the cabs, gave the horses a pat to say thank you, and marched in a grumpy crocodile up to the front door. In fact they looked anything but charming, being dressed in their hideous second-best clothes for travelling. Many of them carried closed matchboxes in their hands.

At home in the country, the Brown family had lots of outdoor animals and most of the animals had fleas, especially the goats. The children had brought with them several fleas, willingly surrendered by the goats, and housed carefully in the matchboxes, lined with animal hair so that they should not feel the journey too badly. They had had an idea that something of the sort might come in useful, at Aunt Adelaide's house: and the moment they set eyes on Pug, they knew they had been right.

Pug and Evangeline led them into the hall, which was very tall and bleak, and they stood round in a resentful circle, longing only to jump back into the four-wheeler cabs, and go home. But Simon gave them a wink and bent down and patted Pug. 'What a dear little dog!' he said. 'Only,' he added, opening his matchbox and giving the contents a shake all over Pug, 'he has fleas.'

The children set up a terrible hullabaloo. 'Ow, ow!' they cried. 'Fleas! Don't let him come near *us*!'

Miss Prawn was overcome with horror and disgust. 'Nonsense! What indelicacy! Dear Pug has no such thing!'

'But look!' said Charlotte, secretly opening *her*

matchbox and pointing to a large flea which had hopped out on to Pug's broad back, and was looking about itself joyfully, hoping Pug would turn out to be a goat.

'Ow, ow!' screamed the children. 'It's another flea!' And they all started scratching like mad and picked up Sugar and Spice and held them out of harm's way. 'Don't let him give fleas to our lovely clean dogs!'

'Pug is perfectly clean,' protested Miss Prawn, scandalized.

'He isn't, he's covered in fleas and now we're covered in fleas too,' cried the children, hopping up and down, scratching themselves. 'And so are you, Miss Prawn – you've got one on your arm.'

And sure enough, a third flea was stretching its hind legs on the fuzzy brown serge of Miss Prawn's sleeve, and this one was quite sure that it was back on a goat. 'Ow, ow, ow!' cried Miss Prawn, and started hopping and scratching too. 'Ow, ow, OW!' cried Evangeline, not even waiting to be flea-ridden before setting up a hullabaloo; and suddenly squealed out: 'Oh, Aunt Adelaide – what do you think? Pug's got fleas!'

For Great-Aunt Adelaide Stitch, ear trumpet and all, had appeared at the turn of the stairs. 'Fleas?' she said, in her high, hooting voice. '*Fleas?*'

'Yes, fleas,' cried the children. 'He's covered in fleas, we're all covered in his fleas, we shall have to go home.' And they started scratching and hopping and wriggling again. Miss Prawn was dancing frantically, holding her arm out stiffly before her, Evangeline wobbling like a jelly with imaginary itching, Sugar and Spice shrilly barking, the wretched Pug lugubriously howling. 'Miss PRAWN!' shrieked Great-Aunt Adelaide into all this tumult. 'What is happening? What's the meaning of this?'

'Pug's got fleas,' yelled the children. They set up a sort of chanting. 'Pug's – got – *fleas*. We'll – all – have to go – home. Pug's – got – *fleas*. We'll – all – have to go – *home* . . .' 'It's fleas,' faltered Miss Prawn. 'On Pug.'

'Fleas?' screeched Aunt Adelaide, over the din. 'I don't believe a word of it. How can he have fleas?'

'It's no fault of mine. He has his weekly bath,' said poor Miss Prawn. She held out a trembling brown serge arm. 'I have one too.'

Aunt Adelaide's eyes nearly popped out of her head. 'I am not interested in your personal habits, Miss Prawn.'

'I didn't mean *I* have a weekly bath,' said Miss Prawn, still holding out her arm.

'Then you ought to. Most insanitary! This is doubtless where all the trouble has arisen. Blaming a poor, innocent little dog, when all the time . . . SILENCE!' yelled Great-Aunt Adelaide suddenly over the hopping and chanting of the children. She descended the stairs, hitting out wildly at the bobbing heads with her ear trumpet. 'Be quiet, all of you! Stop hopping! Nothing serious has happened. No one is going home.' She added in a voice of doom: 'Except Miss Prawn. Prawn, you may depart. You are dismissed.'

Miss Prawn dropped her brown serge arm to her side, flea and all, and stood staring up at Great-Aunt Adelaide, with her face turned as pale as ashes. 'Dismissed? But I can't . . . You can't . . . My poor old mother,' whimpered Miss Prawn, 'she needs the money I give her. And I, myself – where could I go?'

'Wherever you go,' said Aunt Adelaide, 'it will be without a reference.' She gestured majestically up the stairs with her ear trumpet. 'Up to your room and pack your bags! Be gone!'

Absolutely silent, absolutely still, the children watched the meagre figure in its dull brown serge creep up the stairs. But they knew that it couldn't be allowed: they knew that they must confess. What would happen to them when they did, they could not imagine – sent back home in disgrace, poor Mama and Papa recalled from their holiday, Great-Aunt Adelaide ordering out her carriage and galloping round to the lawyer's to alter her will . . . But still, they couldn't let Miss Prawn be sent away. Standing there in their suddenly silent ring, with Evangeline and Pug huddled, scared and miserable, in the middle, the Big Ones exchanged glances: passed the word on silently to the Middling Ones: nodded to the Littlies. Their hearts felt faint and fluttering, but it had to be said. 'Aunt Adelaide –' they began . . .

'Arnk Aggigaige –' said the Baby.

'It isn't Miss Prawn's fault,' said the children. 'You see –'

And there came a knocking at the big front door. And all of a sudden it seemed to open all by itself and someone stood there before it, as it quietly closed. And a voice said: 'The Agency has sent me, Madam. I am Nurse Matilda.'

Chapter 2

AND there she was – Nurse Matilda! – with her bun of hair sticking out at the back of her head like a teapot handle, and her wrinkly round face and two little, black, boot-button eyes. And her nose! – her nose was like two potatoes! She wore a rusty black dress right up to her neck and down to her black button-boots; and a rusty black jacket and a rusty black bonnet all trimmed with trembly black jet. And she carried a very big black stick. What Nurse Matilda could do with that big black stick!

But what you noticed most of all about Nurse Matilda was her Tooth – one huge front Tooth, sticking right out like a tombstone over her lower lip . . .

The children all swung round towards the door and stood there, rooted to the spot, staring. Only the Baby stumbled forward on its fat, bent legs with its nappies falling down, and cried out: 'Nurk Magiggy! Ick my Nurk Magiggy!' The children started to say: 'Yes, it is; it's Nurse Matilda . . .' But somehow the words got stuck in their throats and they found themselves saying to each other instead: '*Who* is it? What is the Baby trying to say?'

All their memories of Nurse Matilda had gone right out of their heads.

But the Baby – the Baby still toddled on; and Nurse Matilda put out a brown, speckled hand and took the Baby's own confiding fat little hand and stood there, holding it. She said to Aunt Adelaide: 'The Agency, Madam, suggested that you might be needing me.' And she looked up at the trembling, brown-clad figure on the stairs. 'To assist Miss Prawn.'

Great-Aunt Adelaide pushed her way through the throng of puzzled children. 'Quite correct. I do indeed need someone. Miss Prawn, however, is leaving.'

Nurse Matilda stood with the Baby's rose-leaf hand in hers. 'I am sorry, Madam. The Agency positively stated that I should assist Miss Prawn.'

She released the Baby's hand and turned to go. 'I
am sorry to have troubled you needlessly.'

'Nonsense!' said Aunt Adelaide. 'You will
remain here.'

'Certainly, Madam – to assist Miss Prawn.'

'Very well, very well,' said Aunt Adelaide,
ungraciously. 'You had better both stay. But I
warn you,' she added, 'Miss Prawn is infested. She

has fleas. She will have to be Dealt With.'

'I shall deal with *every*body, Madam,' said Nurse Matilda; and some sort of shadowy memory seemed to suggest to the children that she probably meant it.

Upstairs, the fleas took one look at the large, chilly rooms set apart for the children, and apparently took a dislike to them; for they hopped back all by themselves into one of the matchboxes and settled down into a little refugee community, grieving for home – which in their case was a large brown goat. The children didn't very much like the rooms either, and they, also, longed for home. Only Miss Prawn seemed blissfully happy to be able to remain with her dear pupil Evangeline, and give Pug his weekly bath.

Nurse Matilda, however, stood no nonsense and soon all the clothes were unpacked and put away in two long dormitories arranged for the boys and the girls; and they collected in Evangeline's schoolroom for tea – which was absolutely horrible, bread and butter and a very solid dark red plum jam, and some extremely dull currant buns. 'After tea,' they said, 'we'll go out into the garden and play some games.'

'After tea,' said Miss Prawn, 'I had thought of a little concert. Evangeline will play her piece –'

'And you will give us one of your songs, Miss Prawn?' cried Evangeline. 'How lovely!'

How ghastly! thought the children; it was gloriously sunny outside.

But Evangeline dashed to the piano and Miss Prawn stepped forward and announced in romantic accents a song called *Prince of My Dreams* and, flinging out her hands towards the children as though inviting them to have a closer look at the

chilblains, opened her mouth. Out of it came a long, high wail like a dog in deep distress.

Miss Prawn, looking somewhat distressed herself, shut her mouth hurriedly; waited a second, opened it again and tried once more. Out came another howl, even higher and longer than the first. Evangeline, banging away at the piano, looked round and nodded encouragement. She evidently thought it all most beautiful.

Sitting cross-legged all round the room, the children stuffed their fists into their mouths to stifle their giggles. For the fact was that Roger had Pug by the tail and was teasing him with a bit of left-over bun.

Pug was a greedy dog and every time the bun disappeared, he howled – and every time it disappeared happened – most strangely – to be

every time Miss Prawn opened her mouth to sing. The poor thing had really got going at last, but she did seem astonished at the sounds that appeared to be coming out of her. 'Pri-hince of my dreeeeeeeams,' she warbled, holding out the chilblains again, and 'Ow-wow-wooooooooow,' wailed Pug. Tears of happiness rolled down Evangeline's cheeks, it was all so beautiful; tears of laughter rolled down the children's, with the effort not to laugh out loud. Sugar and Spice, who couldn't bear music anyhow, opened their mouths and joined in; and Miss Prawn, more and more astounded at the sounds she was making, was evidently beginning to wonder whether she shouldn't have gone in for being an opera singer, after all. Nurse Matilda's beady black eyes looked round upon her charges.

By the end of the song they were beginning to get a little weary of it; the noise really was frightful and it was so nice and sunny out of doors. 'Last chorus!' cried Evangeline, over her shoulder to Miss Prawn, and, 'Thank you, Miss Prawn,' began the children, scrambling to their feet all ready to dash out into the garden the moment it was over.

But it wasn't over. For Nurse Matilda banged just once on the schoolroom floor with her big black stick; and Jennifer found herself, to her own horror, begging: 'Do please sing it again!'

This time Sugar and Spice and Pug needed no urging. They sat in a ring round Miss Prawn and lifted up their heads and howled; and Miss Prawn lifted up *her* head and howled, and Evangeline pounded away at the piano like a mad thing, crimson with happiness at finding her dear Prawny so truly appreciated. 'Pri-hince of my dreeeeeeams,' wailed Miss Prawn and Sugar and Spice and Pug; and, '*Do* sing it once again,' begged Pam: and just couldn't stop herself.

The afternoon passed, the sun was going down; soon there wouldn't be a minute left to go out and play. But on and on sang Miss Prawn and on and on wailed the dogs and the minute it was over, up jumped a child and asked for the song again. Their ears ached, their heads were dizzy with the noise; but on and on it went. However, now they had all been through it and come right down to the Baby. Surely this must be the end? But some old, faint memory told them that it needn't be. Nurse Matilda was quite capable of banging with her stick and starting the whole thing round again. And then round *again* . . .

The Baby stood up. Miss Prawn said, tenderly: 'Prawny sing again for Baby?'

The Baby's round face was very pink, its round blue eyes full of tears. It looked over to where Nurse Matilda stood and said, biting on a trembling lower lip: 'Nurk Magiggy?'

And Nurse Matilda put out her hand to it and suddenly it seemed to the children that her eyes were just a teeny bit less boot-buttony and her nose just a teeny bit less like two potatoes; and all about her was the faintest possible little golden glow. And she said: 'Yes, Baby?'

And the Baby looked over to where Miss Prawn stood exhausted, half proud and yet half hurt and bewildered; and said, 'Poor Prawny!'

And all the children said: 'Yes. It wasn't very nice of us really. We're sorry.'

And Nurse Matilda banged very softly with her big black stick and suddenly . . . Suddenly the sun was shining as though it were only just after teatime, and the children found themselves running gaily down the stairs and out into the garden. 'I do hope,' said Miss Prawn, following

them, hand in hand with Evangeline, 'that they
enjoyed my song.'

'Oh, I'm sure they loved it,' said Evangeline.
'You ought to have given them an encore.'

Chapter 3

W HEN Nurse Matilda came down to breakfast next morning, this is what the children were doing:

Nicholas was touching up Evangeline's chocolate-brown walls with a charming design in porridge.

Christianna had borrowed a needle from the famous work-box and was secretly sewing Evangeline's sleeves to her skirt.

And all the children had taken clothes from Evangeline's wardrobe, and dressed themselves up in them.

Nurse Matilda sat down quietly at the table and said: 'Everyone eat up your porridge.'

'There isn't any porridge,' said the children, looking into the empty bowl.

Nurse Matilda pointed to the pattern of porridge thickly plastered over the walls. 'There is porridge for all,' she said.

The children turned round to the wall and began to try to lick off the porridge. It had got very cold by now and formed into unattractive lumps. By the time it was all gone their faces were quite stiff with porridge, and a rather dreadful grey, and poor Miss Prawn, entering, all eager for a glad new day, gave a shriek of horror and turned and ran out of the room. 'Miss Prawn, Miss Prawn!' cried Evangeline, and tried to run after her; but her mouth was gummed up with porridge and when she lifted her arms her skirts

came too and flapped like the wings of a bat and Miss Prawn only ran faster, haring off down the dark brown corridors shrieking in a piercing voice for help. Evangeline rushed to the door after her and flung out her arms, beseeching her dear Prawny to wait. But of course her sewn-on skirts came up with them again and a swirl of draught sent her sailing off down the corridor like a sand-yacht, and out of sight.

Nurse Matilda banged once on the floor with her big black stick. 'This is the time for Evangeline's Daily Dose,' she said. A very uneasy feeling began to come over the children; some faraway memory told them that when Nurse Matilda banged with her big black stick, you had to go on with whatever you were doing. What if they had to go on wearing Evangeline's clothes (hideous dresses of turkey-red, or purple, with brown Holland overalls and button-boots – the boys were beginning to feel awful fools already) and being treated as though they *were* Evangeline?

And sure enough, they were: for they found themselves lining up and opening their mouths to receive the medicine, one by one. It was horrible medicine: a dingy grey powder, each dose weighed out into a little folded white paper package; but Nurse Matilda relentlessly marshalled each child before her, opened a packet, gave it a tap to loosen the powder, and shook it on to the out-poked tongue. Even the poor Baby, raising its blue eyes imploringly as it stood with its little beak upraised, got a dose. But I'm not sure that it got quite as much as everyone else.

A dreadful hullabaloo from outside drew them to the schoolroom windows. Miss Prawn had reached the garden by now and was fleeing along the neat, sanded paths pursued by a huge navy-blue bat which flapped its wings dreadfully as it ran, uttering muffled cries which sounded like 'Woof! Woof! Woof!' The cries were really only Evangeline, still gummed-up with porridge, calling out to Miss Prawn to stop. But Miss Prawn never paused to look behind her. Across the close-shaven green lawns she sped, leaping with thin, black-stockinged legs over borders and bushes, and after her pounded and bounded Evangeline; and after Evangeline flew Sugar and Spice, and after Sugar and Spice flew Pug, all three yelping, 'Woof! Woof! Woof!' They too had

been at the porridge – but their voices sounded like woof-woof anyway. It didn't make Miss Prawn any happier, all the same.

The children looked with some horror upon this scene; but it was nothing to their horror when a bright voice behind them cried: '*Bonjour, mes enfants.* Now – ze lesson *Française!*' and they realized that their fears were coming all too true. They had dressed themselves up in Evangeline's clothes and now they were going to have Evangeline's French lesson.

And they knew that Evangeline had also been promised by Great-Aunt Adelaide:

Private tuition in
*   elocution,*
*   deportment,*
*   German,*

arms, with the very best intentions in the world they kindly led her off to show her the way.

Of course it wasn't what Mademoiselle had meant at all, but with so many children leading and pushing and pulling her, she could put up very little resistance. '*Laissez moi!*' she cried angrily, and, '*Je ne veux pas! Tais toi!*' But the children couldn't speak French so they only thought she was in a terrible hurry and beseeching them to be quick, and they pushed and pulled even more in their eagerness to get her there in time. Mademoiselle fought and struggled and the more she fought and struggled the more they thought she was in agonies and pushed and pulled her along. But as it was so far and they weren't too sure of the way themselves, they missed it; and soon a little mob had formed, scurrying up and down the twisting corridors with the wretched Mademoiselle in their midst, like a column of ants pushing some large edible object towards the ant-hill: with cries of, 'It's there!' 'No, it isn't – it's that way!' 'No, no, it's round this corner, I'm sure it is . . .' '*Laissez moi!*' protested Mademoiselle, marched to and fro, turned right about and marched back again, run

34

every which way by the children, practically lifted into the air by their kindly hands, with her feet whizzing uselessly under her like the wheels of a clockwork engine picked up off its rails . . . '*Arretez! Laissez moi!* Poot me down!' They did put her down at last, outside the door, and, feeling very proud and helpful, left her there and found their way back to the schoolroom. 'Poor thing!' they said to one another. 'She *was* in a state!'

Mademoiselle was still in a state when she got back. 'Verry well! I go now at vonce to your Tante Adelaide. I tell heem you have bee-have deez-grace-fool. I geeve my noteeze. I quveet.'

She picked up a red velvet bonnet with green velvet streamers and, clapping it back to front on her head in her agitation, marched out of the room: somewhat blinded by the ribbons which hung down in front of her furious face like a rather ragged grass mat.

So from now on, Evangeline might be having private tuition in:

Elocution,

deportment,

German,

Italian, and, above all, the pianoforte. But she would be having no French.

Out in the garden, Miss Prawn had taken refuge behind a little summer-house and crouched there, cowering, while Evangeline prowled about, waving her bat-wings and, in unison with the three dogs, still crying encouragingly through the porridge, 'Woof, woof, woof!'

The tutor who gave Evangeline her German lessons was a kind, stout old gentleman with a huge black beard, called Professor Schnorr – a very good name for him as he was always going to sleep and schnorring like anything. He led the children out into the garden, sat them down in a ring under a little willow tree on the lawn, with German grammars in their hands, sat down himself in a creaky basket-work chair, and without any more fuss went straight to sleep.

The children put down the grammars and watched him thoughtfully. Goodness, he did look hot! Already his poor bald head was becoming quite speckled with pink, as the willow moved its green arms in the breeze and let the sunbeams through. If only he had as much hair on his head as he had on his chin . . .!

'There are some scissors in Evangeline's work-box,' said Caro, thoughtfully.

'And some glue in her writing-desk,' said Lindy.

It was a bit hard to get at the back of his head, but soon Professor Schnorr had a big black beard no longer; but he did have a splendid curly black fringe. As the rest of his head was as bald as an egg, it must be confessed that he looked extremely odd.

And at that moment, several things happened.

Miss Prawn, who had finally been flushed out from behind the summer-house, came scudding round the corner with Evangeline and the three dogs in full cry; from the front door, Mademoiselle (who all this time had been having a lovely time giving in her notice) appeared with a much-enraged Great-Aunt Adelaide; and, standing quietly by a rose bed where nobody had observed her till this moment, the children saw – Nurse Matilda.

At sight of Herr Schnorr, leaping to his feet and tearing out fistfuls of black hair where, up to now, no hair at all had been, Miss Prawn came to a

skidding stop, digging her heels into the gravel so that it flew up into sharp little spurts all around her ankles, Mademoiselle cried out, 'Ooh, *la la!*' and peered with amazement through the green ribbons of her bonnet and Aunt Adelaide advanced down the steps with a look that clearly said, 'This is the end!' Sugar and Spice took advantage of the moment when everyone's attention was elsewhere, to nip Pug smartly in the behind; and Nurse Matilda raised her big black stick.

Down came the stick with a thump and Joanna picked up the scissors and walked over to Sarah and chop, chop, chop, cut off every one of Sarah's curls. 'Ow!' protested Sarah. 'Don't!' But Joanna did; she didn't want to, but somehow she couldn't help it. And before Sarah could cry 'Ow!' again, Sophie had taken the paste-brush and sloshed a little glue on to Sarah's chin; and Hetty had picked up the cut-off curls – and Sarah had a little golden beard. And Sarah had snatched the scissors from Joanna and got to work on Dominic; and Fenella was busy with the paste-pot . . . By the time they came to the Baby, every child was nearly as bald as Professor Schnorr; and every child had a beard. Considering that they were still wearing Evangeline's red and purple dressed and black button-boots, they looked very odd indeed. But snip-snip-snip went the scissors; and slosh-slosh-slosh went the paste: they didn't want to – but they couldn't stop. And now they had come to the Baby.

They stood in a miserable ring and looked at the Baby and the Baby looked back at them, woefully; but the scissors were in Rebecca's hand now and without her even moving her fingers, they seemed to be going snip, snip, snip! 'Stop, stop!' cried everyone, even the children themselves. 'Don't cut the Baby's hair!' 'Nock cucking my hairg!' cried the poor Baby, covering its curly head with two starfish hands. But Rebecca didn't stop. She couldn't stop. Snip, snip, snip went the scissors – she just couldn't help it.

The Baby took one step backward and started to run. Tripping and stumbling over Evangeline's long skirts, it ran. Her boots were far too big for it, of course, and every time it took a step they slewed round and the poor little thing, to its great astonishment, found itself staggering off in quite a different direction. But still it ran: and, staggering and tumbling, tacked across the lawn towards the rose bed and found Nurse Matilda standing there quietly with her big black stick in her hand: and clasped her round her rusty black-skirted knees. 'Nurk Magiggy,' sobbed the Baby. 'Nock wonk my hair cuck!' And it turned and looked round at the children and cried out: 'Kay peag!'

'Please,' cried the children. '*Please*, Nurse Matilda!'

Nurse Matilda stood with the Baby's hand in hers; and – yes! yes! – round her there came that little golden glow; and just for a moment she did look just a little bit less brown and wrinkly, a little bit less boot-button-eyed; a little bit less – well, ugly. And she lifted up her big black stick and gave one thump with it on the grass. And all of a sudden . . .

All of a sudden they were standing there in a ring round Professor Schnorr's creaky basket-work chair; wearing their own clothes and with their own heads of hair, straight or curly, dark or fair – and not a beard amongst them! And Herr Schnorr was as bald as ever he had been. And Miss Prawn and Evangeline were standing quietly by, and Mademoiselle's bonnet was on the right

way round and she no longer peered out through a seaweed of green ribbons. And Nurse Matilda was beside the rose bed with the Baby's hand in hers; and still all about her was that golden radiance.

And Great-Aunt Adelaide Stitch . . .

Great-Aunt Adelaide came graciously down the front door steps towards them. 'Well, children! It appears that you have behaved yourselves today in model fashion. While Evangeline worked quietly with Miss Prawn in the summer-house, the rest, it seems, were exceedingly helpful to Mademoiselle in a matter of some – urgency; and have spent a useful morning under the willow tree with the

Herr Professor. I am exceedingly – gratified,' said Great-Aunt Adelaide, though for a moment it did seem as though she might be going to say 'surprised'. She added: 'As a reward, Nurse Matilda shall take you this afternoon for a visit to Madame Tussaud's Waxworks Show.'

The golden glow round Nurse Matilda suddenly went out.

Chapter 4

SO that afternoon a long line of four-wheeler cabs drew up outside Great-Aunt Adelaide's gate and the children walked down the short drive and all squashed in, the Big Ones with the Middlings perched on their knees, the Middling Ones clasping Little Ones on theirs, and some of the Little Ones even holding Tinies, so that they were piled up in castles of four to a seat. The Littlest Baby and the Littler-Baby-Still had naturally been left at home; but the Baby was there all right, having the time of its life, with its nappies looking as usual as though they were just about to come down: but never quite doing it.

Clip-clop went the sound of the horses' hooves through the London streets and there was a lovely smell of horse, and leather harness and leather-inside-of-cab. The children's heads poked out of the windows like bunches of pleased flowers and the people passing in the horse-drawn omnibuses smiled and waved back at them as they clip-clopped by. The ladies walking along the pavements looked like swans in their long dresses, all billowy with lace ruffles in front, and swirly and bustly at the back, with their big feather hats set forward on their proud heads, their hair piled up high beneath the hats. The gentlemen carried umbrellas, tightly furled; and looked rather like umbrellas themselves in their tight, dark, buttoned-up jackets. But they were all very jolly, it was such a lovely, sunshiny day; and the ladies, also, waved to the children with their gloved hands and the gentlemen flourished their curly bowler hats and it was all very gay.

At last they were at Madame Tussaud's and stood in a long restless line while Nurse Matilda and Miss Prawn counted heads and paid their entrance fees; and then they all rushed in. An Attendant, magnificent in a frogged uniform, stood at the bottom of the grand stairway, smiling helpfully; and Miss Prawn, leaving Nurse Matilda with the Little Ones and the Tinies, beneath a potted palm, tripped over to ask him directions.

The children were up the stairs the moment her back was turned, and shooting down the polished banisters, to the great astonishment of Miss Prawn who, every time she stepped forward to speak to the Attendant, found a child suddenly arriving, apparently out of heaven, between them. She turned away to look for Nurse Matilda; and at that moment Susannah took a corner of the banister too fast and landed slap on top of the Attendant. And what do you think? – the Attendant's head came right off and rolled on the

ground – still smiling politely, however, and with every sign of wishing to do anything he could to help.

'Quick – make a ring round me,' said Sebastian.

So a sort of wall of children formed itself round Sebastian, and when it dissolved there was once again a uniformed figure at the bottom of the stairs, wearing a helpful smile; only of course now it was really Sebastian and not a waxwork at all. Miss Prawn pushed her way back to him. 'Would you direct me please to the History section?' (Even a treat had to be turned by Miss Prawn into lessons; however, you couldn't blame her, with her dear pupil Evangeline lolloping up and down with joy and crying, 'Oh, good! History!')

'History!' groaned the children, turning anxious eyes upon the Attendant. The Attendant said nothing but rolled his eyes towards his left hand which was pointing downwards.

'Down there,' cried the children to Miss Prawn. 'Look, he's pointing down there.'

'Down there' turned out to be the Chamber of Horrors and they all came up again in one minute flat, driven by a pea-green Miss Prawn. 'I said the *History*,' panted Miss Prawn.

As a matter of fact, the History part of the Exhibition would have been lovely if only Miss Prawn had not been quite so keen on imparting information, and her dear pupil Evangeline on airing what she already knew. By the time they came to the Execution of Mary Queen of Scots, the children would very readily have had Evangeline's head upon the block instead of the Queen's.

Poor Mary Queen of Scots, as some children will know, lived – oh, two or three hundred years ago. She thought she ought to be Queen of England too, so Elizabeth, who really *was* Queen of England, had her head chopped off: in those days, this was the great thing to do. So there she knelt, in her black velvet dress, surrounded by nobles and ministers, and there stood the Executioner with his great big axe. 'Wouldn't it be awful if her head really was chopped off, now, here, in front of us?' said Arabella; and Romilly, just to tease Evangeline, said: 'I do believe the Executioner moved.'

'He didn't?' said Evangeline, going pale. 'Yes, he did,' said the children, playing up to Romilly; but at that moment they also went rather pale. For all

of a sudden – the Executioner did move. Up, up, up went the great axe, and very slowly down, down, down it came . . .

For Mary Queen of Scots was not a wax-work at all. It was that wicked Vicky, who had rushed on ahead with Simon and Matthew and Pam and Christopher (when there were so many children, nobody missed three or four at a time). Simon was the Executioner and the others were the nobles and ministers. And down, down, down came the axe – and round a corner came Nurse Matilda with the Little Ones all about her, like a black mother duck with her brood of restless ducklings; and she took one look and she lifted up her big black stick . . .

'Here, hey!' cried Vicky a bit anxiously, screwing round her head to look up at the slowly, slowly descending axe; and, 'Look *out*, Simon!' yelled the children, and 'Ow, ow, ow!' squealed Evangeline, darting round to hide behind Miss Prawn. But on and on, down came the axe. 'Simon, stop it!' screamed the children. But he couldn't stop it. 'Nurse Matilda,' he said, very white and scared, looking over the children's heads to where she stood, '*please!*'

Nurse Matilda looked back at him across the upturned, anxious faces, all turned to look at her now; and she bit on her lip as though – well, honestly, it looked as though she were trying to keep back a smile. And she tapped gently, once, with her stick.

And down came the axe and off flew the Queen's head and landed with a bonk on the floor. But – it wasn't Vicky's head at all: it was a wax head and the ministers and nobles and the Executioner and the Queen herself found themselves back among the rest of the children, placidly looking on. And Miss Prawn was saying, 'Well, now, shall we proceed?' as though nothing had happened.

Nurse Matilda drew near them, her brood of babies around her, all quite unconscious of what had been going on. 'I think, Miss Prawn, that Simon and Victoria are looking a little unwell. Perhaps they had better go down to the hall and sit quietly and wait for us there. Matthew and Pamela and Christopher will go with them. It is a pity they should miss the rest of the treat, but I think they quite understand why.'

Evangeline's mud-colour had by now settled down to her usual rather unlovely pink. Clinging to dear Prawny's hand, she skipped along beside her. 'Now we're coming to the Tiger Hunt, Miss Prawn. Shall I tell about tigers? The tiger is found in the continent of Asia . . .' So eager were they that neither of them noticed three figures slipping along ahead of them . . .

But Nurse Matilda did. 'Antony, Francesca and Teresa will stop handing out rifles this *minute*, please; and come down out of that elephant howdah and join those waiting in the hall . . .'

Down in the hall, Simon, Vicky and the others were having not too boring a time after all. The Attendant was still smiling helpfully at the bottom of the stairs, giving directions to anyone who cared to ask him. Healthy pink faces kept disappearing down below, only to appear looking very unhealthy indeed, protesting that they had asked for Famous Persons or The Tiger Hunt. Elderly lady visitors, demanding to know where they might leave their parasols, were directed to pompous gentlemen visitors, who were enraged to find umbrellas and sixpences pushed into their unwilling hands. A small, stout woman was pointed out to those inquiring for the figure of Queen Victoria, and found herself encircled by a gooping crowd, most of them exclaiming, 'I had no idea she was so ugly!' I can't think *who* had exchanged the two notices saying LADIES and GENTLEMEN.

'It's much more fun down here,' said Matthew and Pam, making room on the bench as they were joined by Antony and Francesca and Teresa. And gosh! they added, here were Joanna and Sarah and Rebecca and Tim. 'You can't think what we found on the way down!' said Sarah. 'A room full of . . .' Even the smiling Attendant came over to hear what they were whispering about.

By the time the visit to Madame Tussaud's Waxworks Show was over, only Miss Prawn and

Evangeline were left up in the galleries, skipping from exhibit to exhibit with squeals of interest and delight; and Nurse Matilda with her brood of baby ducklings, quacking with wonder. In threes and fours, all the rest of the children had been banished to the hall.

But if the children were in the hall – nobody else was. There wasn't even an attendant in sight. Only a horde of children . . .

But what children! Some of them had two heads: some of them had three arms: some of them had as many as six legs, plus their arms and were crawling about among the potted palms, like centipedes; some of them had two or three feet to each leg and were leaping about like frogs. But there wasn't one child that just had one head and two arms and two legs like anybody else.

What Joanna and Sarah and Rebecca and Tim had found on their way down from the gallery was a door; and as the door was marked PRIVATE they had naturally pushed it open and gone through. And what had been behind the door was the room where all the wax heads and legs and arms were kept, for the making and mending of the waxwork figures.

No wonder the hall had so quickly emptied itself!

Miss Prawn took one look at the extraordinary assembly before her, threw up her hands, chilblains and all, and fainted dead away. She landed on top of Evangeline, who, finding herself pinned down by dear Prawny's thin legs and arms, in her bewilderment didn't realize what had happened and thought that she herself had suddenly sprouted extra limbs. With a howl of terror she struggled up and streaked out into the

Marylebone Road, as fast as she could go; and after her went the children in a forest of moving arms and legs. 'Ow, ow, oooooooow!' hooted Evangeline, scudding along the pavements in her black button-boots; and, 'Stop thief!' yelled the naughty children, pounding after her. A policeman, upon hearing this cry, stepped out with upraised hand in Evangeline's path, blowing shrilly on his whistle as he did so. All the dogs in the neighbourhood heard the whistle and came hurrying to see if there was anything going of interest to dogs: towing behind them their reluctant masters and mistresses. Soon Evangeline was surrounded by a dense crowd, insisting upon her being taken into custody at once and deported for life. 'But I haven't stolen *any*thing,' protested Evangeline. 'Look, I've got nothing in my hands. Not in any of them. Oh,' she added, looking down and counting, 'I've only got two now!'

'How many do you usually have?' asked the policeman, coldly.

'Well, I had four a few minutes ago,' said Evangeline.

The crowd immediately changed its mind and

consigned Evangeline to a padded cell instead of the hulks. 'But I did have,' she insisted. 'We all have. The other children have too. Look behind you.'

The crowd turned and looked behind itself. The children, not able to get near Evangeline and rescue her from the dreadful plight they had brought upon her, had been leaping up and down on the outside of the mob, waving their innumerable arms and begging to be heard. At sight of them, the policeman went the colour of dough, flung down his whistle and himself stampeded off down the road, the dogs following,

delighted, towing their owners – all yelling 'Ow, ow, ow!' as loudly as Evangeline herself. And a cab appeared suddenly with Nurse Matilda in it, supporting a tottering Miss Prawn, and whipped up Evangeline and sped on; and there was nothing for the children to do but to start walking home.

You'd think that with all those extra legs it would be easy: but it wasn't. Every time they put a foot down, another foot got in its way and tripped them up; besides, some of the legs were different lengths from their own – the children who had got hold of grown-up legs had to solve it by walking with two on the pavement and one in the gutter, which at least kind of evened out. By the time they arrived at Aunt Adelaide's, they were very hot, weary and hungry children indeed.

But there was no relief even now. *You* just try sitting down when you have two or three extra legs sprouting out of you – there simply isn't room! And when they stretched out their hands for their mugs, the other hands didn't seem to work the same way, but took the mugs and put them back again. And when they reached for bread and butter, one arm was too long and one was too short and neither ever seemed the right length. 'Take your arm out of the way,' they began saying crossly to one another; but they weren't their arms, they were Madame Tussaud's waxwork arms, and Madame Tussaud's arms wouldn't do what the children told them. Soon they were all fiercely squabbling and the noise of all those extra mouths quarrelling had to be heard to be believed . . .

And now the worst thing of all happened. Evangeline, whom they had been laughing at all the afternoon, had appeared in the doorway and was standing there laughing at *them*!

She laughed and she laughed. Her fat cheeks bulged with it, her eyes streamed with tears of delight at their discomfiture. 'All those legs and arms!' squealed Evangeline. 'And how hot and tired and cross you look!'

'Well, all right, Evangeline,' said the children, resentfully. 'We're sorry. We did try to stop them from deporting you for life or sending you to a lunatic asylum, but the crowd wouldn't let us get near you. We were only teasing.'

'Well, now *you're* being teased, aren't you?' said

Evangeline. 'And you jolly well deserve it.' And she began to jump up and down with her arms held out from her sides like a gorilla, chanting, 'La la four legs! La la two heads!' in a very silly and offensive voice.

But . . . It was a funny thing: was there or was there not growing behind Evangeline a sort of – radiance? 'Evangeline,' said the children, 'why are you – well, kind of shining?'

'Am I?' said Evangeline, surprised. But she looked round, over her shoulder. 'Oh,' she said. 'It isn't me. It's Nurse Matilda.'

'What are you doing here, Evangeline?' said Nurse Matilda.

'Teasing the children,' said Evangeline. 'Don't they look silly?'

'Yes, they do,' said Nurse Matilda. 'But they also look very miserable.'

'Well, it serves them right for being beastly to me,' said Evangeline, and began capering up and down again.

'Once people have said sorry,' said Nurse Matilda, 'that is the end of it.'

'Not with me, it isn't,' said Evangeline. 'I expect I shall go on doing this for *hours*.'

'I dare say you will,' said Nurse Matilda, very quietly; and she banged twice with her big black stick.

I don't know how long Evangeline had to go on leaping up and down, chanting, 'La la – four legs!' but certainly the children heard her still at it

as, bathed and nightgowned, teeth cleaned, prayers said and tucked into their beds at last, each with their own two arms and no more, and their own two legs and no more – they laid their heads (one apiece) on their pillows and went off to sleep.

Those extra heads and legs and arms must have got back somehow to Madame Tussaud's. I suppose Nurse Matilda saw to that.

Chapter 5

S O the days went by. There was lots to do in London, afterall, and on the whole the children were busy and happy and therefore reasonably good – if only because they were getting a bit wary about Nurse Matilda banging with her big black stick and making them go on being naughty. They went out into the park, walking two by two in a long crocodile (kept tidy by the wretched Prawn, who had to keep scudding up and down poking them back into place with her parasol) and to the exhibition at the Crystal Palace – they might have had a good time there, keeping very still and pretending to be statues, but most of the statues had nothing on and they weren't prepared to go as far as that. And they went to the Tower and pretended to Evangeline that they were going to feed Pug to the ravens, and to Kew Gardens where they abandoned her in a hot-house and she ran round and round searching for them, scarlet in the face and with perspiration breaking out all over her. And at Hampton Court they lured poor Prawn into the maze and then just kept terribly quiet so

that she thought they had all got out and left her there: and ran about like a very thin hen, distractedly clucking at the top of its voice for its chicks. And they went to the Penny Bazaar in Soho Square, and I'm sure you will all be very glad to know that what they did there, was to put all their pennies together and buy a present for Miss Prawn. It was a pink satin handkerchief-sachet with 'pen-painting' on it: a very lumpy pattern of forget-me-nots, done with oil paint splodged on with a nib. I think Miss Prawn would probably have remembered the children's visit anyway, without the aid of forget-me-nots; but she had received so little kindness in her rather bleak life that she was quite overwhelmed by the gift and, blinded by tears of emotion, banged into a door-post and had to be led home and put to bed. So perhaps it would have been better if they hadn't given it to her after all.

And then there were the lessons. Thanks to Nurse Matilda, Herr Schnorr and Mademoiselle appeared to have forgotten all about their earlier meetings; and they now plied the children with German and French; Signora Cabbargio (rightly so called, because that is exactly what she looked like) plied them with Italian, and Mr Smink, who gave Evangeline lessons in deportment and elocution, plied them with deportment and elocution. They had to watch first while Evangeline paraded the room with a board tied to her back: it seemed to serve no useful purpose but certainly made her look the most extra-ordinary shape. However, it wasn't so funny when they had to do it themselves; and then they formed into a ring and had to skip round pretending to be elves and fairies. This was mercifully interrupted by a footman arriving, chalk-white, with a message from Great-Aunt Adelaide that the house was to be abandoned at once and everyone to take to the open spaces, as England had evidently been visited, for the first time in history, by an earthquake. She herself was found hours later, flat on her face in a field. The children really felt very sorry when they saw how shaky she looked, and a bit crestfallen too, at finding London still in one piece; and wished they had given *her* the pink handkerchief-sachet. However, they had no money left. 'We could do a concert for her,' suggested Stephanie.

'Ooh, yes!' cried Evangeline, skipping with joy and nearly bringing on an earthquake all of her own. 'And I could do my recitation.'

The children were not too keen about Evangeline's recitation – they had heard it a good many times already. It was a poem of great power and beauty which she had actually made up herself, about a little girl who steals jam from the larder and causes her dear Mama to shed a tear. But so hard-hearted and lost to virtue is the little girl that the tear dries up, and for the rest of her life she seems to be wandering around looking for this wasted tear of her dear Mama's. Evangeline really let herself go on the last bit when she had grown into quite an old woman, still doddering about with an imaginary stick, looking for the tear; and finally expiring, worn out and dejected, with a loud thump on the schoolroom floor, to the great admiration of Mr Smink her elocution teacher and the great relief of everyone else.

However, if Evangeline could make up poems so could they, and there was a great deal of muffled squeaking and giggling in corners as they thought up some contributions of their own. Miss Prawn would be having her evening off and was taking Nurse Matilda to visit her Mama. Her Mama was in fact a horrid old thing who took all Miss Prawn's meagre earnings and spent them on cheese, of which she was inordinately fond. Miss Prawn, however, was devoted to her and dashed round at every spare moment with even more presents of cheese. But it meant that fortunately nobody would be there who would really *hear* the poems. 'We can arrange something about Aunt Adelaide's ear trumpet,' said the children.

So that evening after supper they all trooped down to the drawing-room, where Aunt Adelaide was sitting in a chair of state, with Parrot in his cage on one side of her and Canary on the other, and Pug at her feet; all quite excited at the treat in store.

Of course Evangeline went first. Arrayed in one of the turkey-red dresses, with yellow blodges all over it this time, she stood up, as taught in Mr Smink's deportment lessons, shoulders well back – which unfortunately meant stomach well out – hands hanging limply at her sides like small underdone suet puddings. Aunt Adelaide clapped her own horny hands together, Parrot screeched 'Anchors aweigh!' which was all this very dull bird could say. Evangeline dipped a curtsy, one foot crumpling uncomfortably behind her, and announced: 'THE LOST TEAR.'

'What, dear? Can't hear,' said Aunt Adelaide,

leaning forward like a one-horned cow, the trumpet stuck in her ear.

'THE LOST TEAR,' bellowed Evangeline, and began.

'Oh, list to me while I do tell
What to a girl called Maria befell.
It is a tale I fear most sad
Because Maria turned out bad.'

'Bravo, bravo!' cried Great-Aunt Adelaide, waving the ear trumpet, apparently under the impression that this was the end. It by no means was, but she was delighted to discover it. She was not of a literary turn herself and could not get over Evangeline having made it up. Standing behind her chair, Mr Smink gestured encouragement. Evangeline continued.

'This girl her happiness did sell
Because her mother made some jell-
Y and did leave it on the shelf.
She did not say, "Help yourself."
'But Maria to that shelf did come.
At first she took only some.
But soon there was no longer plenty
For the pot of jam was empty.'

Behind Great-Aunt Adelaide, Mr Smink peered into an imaginary pot, living again the part of Mama at the moment of discovery. Evangeline also lifted hands in horror and put on a dreadfully long face.

' "Alas, where did that jelly go,
My dear Maria, do you know?"
Oh, listeners! – what must I relate?
I do not like to say it quite.
' "Speak out! To your Mama reply!"
Listeners! – Maria told a lie.
A lie she told Mama I fear.
Her poor Mama did shed a tear . . .'

And so they had come at last to the lost tear

and after about eleven more verses Evangeline (and Mr Smink) had grown old and feeble, doddering about gooping into pretence corners, looking for the wasted tear; and they were able to rush forward and raise the large lump of Evangeline where she lay expiring on the floor, and with many bows share Aunt Adelaide's loud applause. Agatha seized the opportunity to remove a piece of toffee from her gums where she had been nursing it all this time, and stuff it as far as it would go down Aunt Adelaide's ear trumpet.

Mr Smink departed, exhausted, and the next part of the concert began. Jennifer – rather terrified now that they had really got to the point – stood up and gabbled off a poem she had made up about Great-Aunt Adelaide herself –

'Great-Aunt Adelaide, she bought a woolly coat,
She grew a little beard and she thought she was a
goat.
The children started laughing, they thought it was so
silly,
She didn't seem to KNOW if she was a Nanny or a
Billy.'

This was very well received by the children

except for Evangeline who burst into loud boo-hoo-hoos and said she would tell Aunt Adelaide. However, it was very hard to tell Aunt Adelaide anything because of the toffee in her ear trumpet. To punish Evangeline for being so sneaky, Helen leapt up and did one about Miss Prawn –

'Poor Miss Prawn's so skinny and skimpy,
When she floats in her bath she looks more like a
*   shrimpy.'*

The children thought this was funnier than ever, especially the Little Ones who turned it into a song and hopped up and down chanting it, like a lot of miniature Red Indians; which quite drowned Evangeline's efforts to bellow into the ear trumpet that the horrid children were being disrespectful. 'I'll do one about Mr Smink,' said Louisa –

'Mr Smink, what do you think? –
When he takes off his boots his feet do –'

'Louisa!' screamed the children, divided between horror and hilarity. 'Now Gumble,' said Quentin.

So Megan did one about Gumble –

'Gumble, the butler, 'e
Sat on some cutlery;

Goodness, he did feel sore!
The knives, forks and spoons
Inflicted such wounds
That he'll never sit down no more.'

This, however, was too much for the Baby; it couldn't bear the idea of poor Gumble not being able to sit down. Rhiannon had to make up one about Fiddle, to help it forget –

'Poor old Fiddle
She danced on a griddle,
But it was dreadfully hot.
So, right in the middle,
She did a great w –'

'Rhiannon!' screamed all the children again.

'– *which cooled it down a lot,'* finished Rhiannon triumphantly.

This one had almost as fatal an effect, for it reduced the Baby to such a paroxysm of giggling that it had to be picked up and hugged and shaken and beaten on the back. I'm afraid Fiddle's sufferings were quite lost, in the Baby's delight in a grubby joke.

Encouraged by its ecstatic chuckling, Sally made up another one –

'Professor Schnorr, he took off his vest

But — it was rather rummy —
His beard was so huge that it covered his chest
And even a bit of his tummy —'

and this reduced it to such a state of helplessness that they had to leave it to recover and do one about Evangeline's Intended, Adolphus Haversack —

'When Adolphus was a little boy, his Ma went to the
Zoo with him,
She went to the Head Keeper and she asked what
they could do with him.
She said, "Please keep Adolphus, and I'll pay an
honorarium,"
But they thought she said "a dolphin" and he's
now in the aquarium.'

This was the end for Evangeline, who gave a great howl of rage, seized Aunt Adelaide's trumpet and began angrily hitting out with it at whatever child came nearest. A great deal of shouting and ow-ow-ow-ing ensued, Parrot joining in with raucous cries of 'Anchors aweigh!', Canary shrilling, Sugar and Spice nipping away at Pug, till all the air was filled with tufts of brown hair: ow-ow-ow-ing pretty loudly themselves as Pug nipped back. Great-Aunt Adelaide, not able to

ignore the fact that it was Evangeline who had
started the trouble and, anyway, wanting to get
her ear trumpet back, swiped out at her with the
cushion of her chair, which burst into a fine
flurry of feathers. If Aunt Adelaide could wage a
pillow-fight, so could the children, and they all
snatched up cushions and laid about them too.
Some of the feathers floated down into the ear
trumpet and got glued up with the toffee, and
soon a sort of bird's nest had formed there, into
which Canary flew and sat serenely singing. Even
Aunt Adelaide could hear the trilling, muffled
though it might be with feathers and toffee, when

she had finally wrested back the ear trumpet from Evangeline; and she thought something must have gone seriously wrong with her hearing, and began to ring the bell for someone to go and fetch the doctor. The Baby, who had decided that its own turn had come, had meanwhile climbed laboriously on to a chair and now stood there, rather mournful because nobody would listen to its party piece. The room was in pandemonium, so thick with fur and feathers and the sound of dogs barking, Canary shrilling, children laughing, Evangeline howling, Aunt Adelaide exclaiming and Parrot shrieking 'Anchors aweigh!' that nobody heard the door open; until into the bedlam Nurse Matilda's voice said: 'You rang, Madam?' and suddenly silence fell.

Great-Aunt Adelaide held out the ear trumpet. 'I have a curious singing in my ears.'

Nurse Matilda took the ear trumpet, poked down a curled forefinger and hooked out the bird's nest, Canary and all. 'Well, there! I can hear perfectly again,' said Aunt Adelaide, greatly astonished. She glanced round the room somewhat uncertainly. 'We have had a delightful entertainment, Nurse. Charming.'

'Evidently, Madam,' said Nurse Matilda; and she lifted up her big black stick.

From the chair, the Baby held out its fat hands. 'Nurk Magiggy! Nurk Magiggy!' And, pleased to have the attention of its audience at last, it made an unsteady bob curtsy. The children looked at it with love and pity. What could it possibly know, poor little thing, that it could perform?

'Kinging ge Goognike Kong,' said the Baby.

So they all stood round and sang with the Baby the song that their mother used to sing to them as she tucked them up in bed . . .

'Mama must go now,
 Time for your bed now,
 On your white pillow
 Lay your little head now.
'The dark is a friend, so
 We'll turn out the light.
 Today's at an end, so
 Darlings, good night!'

Great-Aunt Adelaide sat quietly, the cow's-horn of her ear trumpet bent forward to listen to the children's voices. When the singing was over, Nurse Matilda let her black stick down very gently to the floor, without any bang at all. 'Very

Ma – ma must go now, time for your bed now;

On your white pil-low lay your lit-tle head now.

The dark is a friend, so we'll turn out the light,

To-day's at an end, so dar - lings, good night!

well, children,' she said. 'We will now go upstairs. The Big Ones will remain to clear up, and then follow.' And she lifted up the Baby and, holding it in the crook of her arm, gave Aunt Adelaide a respectful little bob. 'Good night, Madam. Good night, Miss Evangeline.'

'Good night, Nurse,' said Great-Aunt Adelaide; and she added to Evangeline, 'An ill-favoured woman. But just this evening – didn't you think she looked somewhat less – homely?'

'And all goldeny,' said Evangeline. 'I've noticed it before.'

Chapter 6

ONE day, Nurse Matilda said to the children: 'I have a message from your Great-Aunt Adelaide. Tomorrow evening, she is giving a soirée. A soirée is an evening party. Your Great-Aunt Adelaide wishes the older children to be present, in their best clothes. The rest will go to bed at the usual time.'

'Oh, no!' groaned all the children. The Big Ones didn't want to go to Aunt Adelaide's soirée (or anywhere else) in their best clothes, and the Little Ones didn't want to go to bed at the usual time.

The next morning, when the children came in from their half-hour of Healthful Fresh Air before breakfast, this is what they had been doing:

Daniel had pinned up a large notice at the Tradesmen's entrance, saying: INFECTOUIS DISEESE, NO ADMITTENS. Hannah had

mixed some of the schoolroom chalk with water and filled up all yesterday's milk-bottles with it.

Tora had painted little red spots on the glass pane of the big front door.

The other children had dug up lots of worms in case they might come in useful, at Aunt Adelaide's soirée.

Cook became more and more mystified as the morning wore on and no butcher or baker or fishmonger arrived with their goods for that evening's party. 'Drat them tradesmen!' she said to Nurse Matilda, over their elevenses in the Servants' Hall. 'And the extra help hasn't come either. But I must say, your young ladies and gentlemen are being very helpful. I never did see such children for helpfulness.'

The children were indeed being very busy assisting with preparations for Great-Aunt Adelaide's soirée.

Jaci had made a little hole in the bottom of the kettle and every time Cook put it on the range, in two minutes it was empty and the fire underneath had gone out.

Hetty was standing beside Cook as she made her sausage rolls, and as fast as Cook filled one, she prodded the sausage out and put it quietly back with

81

the rest. ('I must have mistook me quantities,' said Cook, looking with dismay at the undiminished pile of sausages still waiting to be wrapped round with pastry.)

Sophie was curling the worms up lovingly on the little chocolate cakes.

Justin had opened the sandwiches and was putting in a teeny thin layer of wet cotton wool; and closing them up again.

Toni had filled up the coffee tin with earth.

Arabella had wrapped a crêpe bandage round the fruit cake and covered the whole thing with icing.

Clarissa had folded a yellow duster in with the sponge roll and Cook was quite happy, thinking it was apricot jam.

Agatha had sewn together the knees of Gumble's best evening trousers, and the hem of Fiddle (the parlourmaid's) dress.

Sebastian had filled the toes of their shoes with a stiff greengage jelly.

All the other children were helping with Great-Aunt Adelaide's party too.

And that afternoon, by great good fortune, as they were playing about in the garden, who should arrive but Signora Cabbargio, all eager for the fray. She was going to sing at the soirée, and was in a great state because she couldn't find anyone to translate her Italian song into English. The children were only too happy to help her and soon she was practising away, under the willow tree, at a song which largely consisted of the words, 'La Great-Aunt Adelaide-a, Ees a seely old fool-a . . .'

And so the evening of the party came. The younger ones were put to bed and immediately got up again and cautiously scuttled downstairs. The Big Ones resentfully climbed into their best clothes – the girls in white embroidered dresses, half-way down their calves and dreadfully scratchy with starch, the boys in white sailor suits with their trousers half-way down *their* calves. I must say they looked hideous; but Evangeline far outshone them in a dress of an incredibly nasty green with lemony squirls all over it. Great-Aunt Adelaide herself was resplendent in purple satin; with her hair – and a lot of false hair too – piled up in large lumps and blobs on top of her head, rather as though someone had been making mud-pies there and just left them. Stuck in among the mud-pies were lots of combs and feathers, and dropped in among the feathers by Susie, although Aunt Adelaide did not know it, were some monkey nuts. Parrot was very fond of monkey nuts.

Aunt Adelaide also did not know that behind every chair and curtain and under every table, were hidden small and middling children, already in the last stages of muffled giggling.

Gumble and Fiddle had been given a light snack by Cook before the party began, as the tradesmen hadn't arrived with their proper supper. They had had a fearful time with the cotton-wool sandwiches, chewing away like goats but getting no further, and it had made them late for everything. They were still struggling into their clothes as the first bell rang, and with great shrieks of 'They're here!' and 'My feet!' and 'Drat it!' (from Cook, who had been having an anxious time too, because the decorations on her little chocolate cakes simply wouldn't stay still) – they hastened out into the hall. But what with the legs of Gumble's trousers having been stitched together at the knees, and the hem of Fiddle's skirt being sewn into a bag, it ended in a sort of sack race: all the worse because the jelly in their shoes kept oozing out, squidge, squidge, round their ankles as they hopped and lolloped to the front door and peered through the glass pane at the first arrivals.

You remember that Tora had that morning painted the glass all over with little red spots?

The first guests were, in fact, Sir Choppup de Lot and his Lady. Sir Choppup de Lot was a famous foreign surgeon. He had chopped up Aunt Adelaide's late husband right, left and centre, and although she had immediately become a widow, she had great faith in him. But now . . . 'Goot heavints!' exclaimed Sir Choppup, peering in through the glass as Gumble peered out. 'Vot eest mit de bootlaire? He iss covet mit spots!'

And at the same moment, Gumble cried out: 'Oh, my goodness! Sir Choppup and her ladyship! Spots all over them!'

Fiddle was in a terrible taking. 'Measles! Chicken-pox! Come over them sudden in the kerridge as they was driving here!' and off she went, hop, hop, squidge, squidge, to the drawing-room to tell Madam: entering with a last flying leap most upsetting to the nerves of Great-Aunt

Adelaide Stitch. 'What on earth is the matter, Fiddle? Control yourself!'

'People with spots, Madam!' gasped Fiddle, exhausted with emotion and hopping. 'Trying to get in!'

'People with spots?' cried Aunt Adelaide. 'This is not an Isolation Hospital. Drive them away!'

'Drive them away: Madam says, drive them away!' cried Fiddle, bounding back into the hall.

'Go away, go away!' echoed Gumble obediently, making violent shoo-ing gestures through the glass.

'Gone out of hiss mindt,' said Sir Choppup, quietly. 'Med! Ravink!' And he took Lady de Lot by the arm and led her down the steps again. 'Be prepart for bat newss, my dear! Be brave! Mit spots, and ravink med: I know ter signs. It iss ter Plague.'

'The Plague?' squealed Lady de Lot. A second carriage had just bowled in through the gate and she rushed to it. 'Don't stop, drive off, save yourselves! The house is stricken with the Plague!' And she leapt into her own carriage after Sir Choppup and they never stopped until they came to Dover; and there took the Ostend packet, leaving all their possessions behind, and were never heard of in England again. Wasn't it sad for them?

Gumble, meanwhile, had got the front door open and as there was now no spotted glass between them, he admitted the next lot of guests without further trouble and they were able to tell Aunt Adelaide all about the lunatics they had met, who had burbled to them about the Plague and rushed off into the night. From under the tables and behind the sofas and chairs, the children listened and nearly split themselves with laughing.

By ten o'clock most of the guests had arrived, graciously received by Great-Aunt Adelaide, complete with mud-pie hair-do, combs, feathers, Parrot and all – for Parrot had found the nuts by now and unknown to Great-Aunt Adelaide was happily scrabbling about for them on top of her head; and Gumble and Fiddle were free of the front door and able to hurry about offering trays of refreshment. The stitching had come apart and they no longer had to proceed in kangaroo hops and bounds, but the jelly oozing out of their shoes was proving a great attraction to Pug and Sugar and Spice, who followed them about devotedly. Susie had tied the loose end of a reel of black cotton to the tail of each dog. The cotton was forming a splendid web of almost invisible thread about the legs of the guests, as the dogs wove their way between them, trailing Fiddle and Gumble.

Evangeline stood smugly at Great-Aunt Adelaide's side, bobbing a curtsy to each new guest, holding her hands out, bent at the wrists, in an excessively silly and affected way. 'We'll soon put an end to *that*,' said the children; and snip, snip went a pair of scissors through the buttons and

bows at Evangeline's back and brrrrrrp! went
the elastic of Evangeline's knickers ... 'Good
evening, Ma'am! How d'ye do, Ma'am,' piped
Evangeline, bobbing her fiftieth curtsy; and
suddenly whoops! went Evangeline's pants, down
round her ankles. She gave a stout wriggle and
surreptitiously hauled them up, but the next guest
was upon her. 'Evangeline, your curtsy!' hissed
Great-Aunt Adelaide. 'Yes, Aunt,' said Evangeline,
wretchedly bobbing – and whoops! down they
came again. All round the room, the drawn

curtains shook and bellied with the ecstasy of the Middling Ones and the Little Ones, trying to stifle their laughter.

At ten o'clock came a great moment – the arrival of Mr and Mrs Haversack and Adolphus. Adolphus was the young man chosen by Great-Aunt Adelaide to marry Evangeline when she should be old enough.

The guests had been having a rather puzzling time with the earth coffee and hollow sausage-rolls – (fortunately, perhaps, none of the little chocolate cakes would stay still long enough for anybody to eat one) – and were quite glad to stop enjoying the light refreshments and turn to watch the great entry. 'My dear Adelaide – so delighted!' cried the guests of honour, advancing upon their hostess with outstretched hands . . .

Or trying to advance: for by this time the whole room was a network of knee-high black thread, and they found themselves to their great astonishment, flung back and out in the hall again. 'Come in, my dears, come in!' begged Aunt Adelaide, surprised, trying to surge forward in her turn, to meet them. But she too was flung back with a jerk, and Parrot, dozing among the combs and feathers on her head, lost his balance and gave a shrill shriek of 'Anchors aweigh!' '*What*, dear?' cried the Haversacks, appearing in the doorway and disappearing backwards into the hall again, as the black threads caught them across their knees. Between hall and drawing-room, Gumble stood ankle-deep in greengage jelly, a look of numbed bewilderment on his face.

At the far end of the room, Signora Cabbargio had meanwhile burst into song, holding the children's translation at arm's length as she blissfully warbled away. 'La Great-Aunt Adelaide-a, Ees a seely old fool-a,' carolled Madame Cabbargio. Great-Aunt Adelaide caught her own name now and again and graciously bowed and smiled. She observed with quiet satisfaction that her guests seemed quite spellbound by the beauty of the song: standing with bent heads, staring down at their toes, purple with suppressed emotion.

Away at the door, Mr and Mrs Haversack were still beating back and forth at the web of cotton stretched across the doorway, as though thrown up on a shore and sucked back again by heavy seas. 'Come in, come in!' hooted Great-Aunt

Adelaide, high-stepping towards them over the mesh, Parrot clinging for dear life to the mud-pies, Evangeline following, clinging for dear life to the legs of her knickers. 'We can't!' cried Mr and Mrs Haversack, despairing. The guests stood gaping, torn between horror and joy. The hidden children held their aching tummies and could hardly bear to laugh any more.

Fortunately, at this moment Signora Cabbargio ended her song and, bowing right and left to the applause, barged her way like a triumphant elephant out of the room, the network smashed and trampled before her enormous progress. Her going left a pathway, through which Mr and Mrs Haversack could at last advance. Adolphus bowed and lifted Evangeline's hand to his lips. She let go for a moment: and whoops! down came one leg.

Sally, who all this time had been nursing Evangeline's canary for just the right occasion, decided that it had come. The canary gave a happy chirrup at being set free, and flew softly down and settled in Mr Haversack's beard. Everything about Mr Haversack was expensive – even his beard was golden; the canary was just the same colour and in a moment invisible.

'Evangeline,' commanded Aunt Adelaide. 'Your curtsy!'

'I can't,' mumbled Evangeline, anxiously hauling on the fallen knicker-leg. And anyway, the time was approaching for her party-piece. 'I must go,' she muttered and, giving one last desperate hitch, walking stiffly like a prisoner in leg-irons, she crept away.

'Poor child, she is unwell. Mr Haversack and I will overlook it. Will we not, my dear?' said Mrs Haversack, all gracious kindliness. But Mr Haversack himself seemed not, entirely well, for his beard began to fluff itself up in a really alarming manner and he answered only in a series of shrill little chirps. 'He has had no dinner; we were delayed,' said Mrs Haversack, looking at him anxiously. 'A crumb to eat, perhaps?' A crumb in fact would have been just the thing, or even some bird-seed; but she espied Fiddle, squelching round with a delicious-looking jam roll. 'A slice of this, perhaps? Haversack is so fond of apricot; aren't you, my dear?'

Mr Haversack burst into a prolonged chirruping, quite as astonishing to himself as to his neighbours. Mrs Haversack sawed at the

yellow duster rolled into the sponge. The children shook and sobbed with laughter, and almost longed for it to end.

The miserable Evangeline, meanwhile, had climbed up on to the small dais prepared, tightly gripping the sides of her skirts, and now announced THE LOST TEAR, and dropped a curtsy. Nothing else dropped this time as, in holding on to her dress she was also holding up her pants.

'*Oh, list to me while I do tell*
 What to a girl called Maria befell –'
'Beautiful, beautiful!' said Mrs Haversack.

'She made it all up herself,' said Great-Aunt Adelaide, proudly.

'Prrrrrrrr-up,' said Mr Haversack's beard.

From his corner, poor Mr Smink gazed upon his pupil in despair, as the poem progressed. For where was the note of pathos which they had so devotedly rehearsed together? Where were the actions, the telling gestures? The imaginary kitchen table with Mama using both hands to make an imaginary pot of jelly . . . The high shelf, with Maria reaching up both hands to take down the imaginary pot and gollop up the lot . . . ' "Alas! —" ' prompted Mr Smink, violently signalling from his corner, throwing up both arms in horror as Mama discovers the loss of the jam; but Evangeline only turned upon him a look of anguish and, with her hands glued to her sides, ploughed on.

The children were so hysterical with laughter that the Big Ones had to creep in with the others, under the tables and chairs and behind the curtains, to hide themselves from the grown-ups . . . The younger Ones were quite sick with it already, doubled up with giggles; and under the huge centre table, the Baby was being very silly, marching up and down with its nappies trailing, rather bent because the table wasn't quite high enough, and reciting Evangeline's poem in its own language. Every now and then it collapsed in a small heap of squeaking giggles and then, encouraged by the helpless laughter of the rest, staggered up and was off again. The children rocked and rolled and burst with laughter, hugging their aching tummies, begging it to stop; but so much success had gone to its head and off it went again. After a bit, other children crawled across from other tables and chairs and sofas, and soon there was a sort of encampment under the big middle table. And then more children came and more, and the long table-cloth began to bulge and heave with so many of them being there, and all of them rolling about with laughter.

It was really extraordinary that the grown-ups didn't discover them . . .

Very extraordinary . . .

They lifted up the edge of the table-cloth and peered out between the bobbles.

There weren't any grown-ups there any more. While they had laughed and laughed, and cried with laughter – the party had ended, the guests had all gone home. 'Thank goodness,' said the children, crawling out from under the table, hugging their aching tummies, wiping their streaming eyes. 'We can stop laughing now and go up to bed . . .'

But Nurse Matilda stood in the doorway; and she lifted her big black stick and gave one bang with it on the drawing-room floor: and the children began to laugh again.

They laughed and they laughed. The tears ran down their faces and their cheeks ached and their tummies ached, but they couldn't stop it; and if they even seemed to begin to stop, one of them would say, 'Fly at once, it iss ter Plague!' and off they would go again; and if that began to dry up, another would warble, 'Seely old fool-a,' or the Baby would stagger up and start stumping up and down imitating Evangeline; or they would all start thinking about the yellow-duster jam roll. Or if they really did seem to be recovering at last, someone would cry out: 'Whoops!' and they would all fall about into paroxysms of hysteria once more.

They laughed and they laughed. They longed to stop, but they couldn't stop. They were worn out with it, exhausted with it, longing to end it; but they couldn't . . . All over the house, the lights would be going out, Evangeline, worn out with her triumphs would be fast asleep in bed, Great-Aunt Adelaide would be taking off some of the mud-pies, combing the nutshells out of the rest; Fiddle and Gumble would be shaking the last of the jelly out of their shoes . . . But *they* must laugh and laugh – aching with it, sobbing with it, rolled up against one another in an absolute agony; praying, 'Oh, let it stop! Let it stop!'

Nurse Matilda stood in the doorway and watched them. 'Oh, Nurse Matilda,' they cried, 'do let us stop!' And they said to the Baby, 'You ask her, Baby. Go to Nurse Matilda and ask her to bang with her stick again, and let us stop.'

The Baby sat in a round, doleful bundle

beneath the big table, its blue eyes brimming with tears of giggling, but longing only to go to its little bed. 'Carnk,' it said. 'Koo karg!'

'Oh, poor little thing!' cried the children. 'It's too tired.' And they picked it up and staggered with it over to Nurse Matilda. 'Please, Nurse Matilda, just let the Baby off. Never mind us, if you'll let the Baby off.'

'Ah,' said Nurse Matilda. 'That's better, isn't it?' The Baby stood rocking with weariness before her and she stooped down and lifted it up in her arms; and in that mo-ment it was asleep, its head on her rusty black shoulder.

And the children weren't laughing any more. They stood all around her, quietly, and she said to them – quietly – 'Sometimes what amuses us is rude and hurtful to others: isn't it?' And without another word, still carrying the sleepy Baby in her arms, she led them out into the hall and up the broad staircase and said: 'All go to bed now. And no noise, please. No giggling.'

The children went to bed. They made no noise and you can be sure there was no giggling. But they did say just a few words to one another before they went off to sleep. 'When Nurse Matilda smiles,' they said, 'just for a moment – doesn't she look pretty?'

Chapter 7

AND so the days went by and, worn out perhaps by the really enormous amount of naughtiness they had expended on Great-Aunt Adelaide's soirée, the children went quite gaily along with hardly any outbreaks. They went to the Zoo and, apart from shutting Evangeline into an empty monkey cage (to the delight of the neighbouring monkeys who kept pressing bits of bun on her, squeezing them through the bars) – and joining a crocodile of convent school-children, to the great mystification of the nuns in charge, who suddenly found themselves with twice as many pupils as they had started out with – they really behaved very well. True, they did once change Aunt Adelaide's great flowered hat back to front, and she drove through the park bowing graciously to

her friends, all unaware that she looked as though someone had sewn a packet of mixed seeds on her forehead; but she never knew, so perhaps it hardly counted? And they did label a large bar of yellow soap 'Cheese', and send it off to Miss Prawn's horrid old mother; but actually it was rather a success, so we needn't count that either. (She was so greedy that she ate her way steadily through it and by the end acquired quite a taste for it. At first Miss Prawn was much alarmed as she approached their little house, to see bubbles floating out of the dining-room window; but she soon got used to finding the old lady in a rich white lather and the soap was cheaper so I'm glad to say in the end she saved quite a lot of money.) But really one can say that they were pretty good, and Nurse Matilda took them to all sorts of interesting places and told them stories and read to them and she seemed to get prettier and more smiley every day, and on the whole they were having a lovely time, when –

When –!

When one afternoon, Nurse Matilda came to the schoolroom and said: 'Your Great-Aunt

Adelaide is entertaining a friend to tea. Her name is Mrs Green. You are to wash your hands and faces and put on your best clothes and go down and meet her.'

'How lovely!' cried Evangeline, hastening off with Miss Prawn to choose yet another of her ghastly dresses. 'How awful!' began the children. But they took one look at the big black stick and said instead, 'Yes, Nurse Matilda,' and went down quietly as they had been told and sat down in a ring round Great-Aunt Adelaide and Mrs Green. And Mrs Green said, 'I never *saw* such well-behaved children.'

'Aren't they?' said Great-Aunt Adelaide. Their behaviour had certainly improved of late and she thought it was all due to the virtuous example set them by her dear Evangeline.

'When I left home,' said Mrs Green, 'this is what *my* children were doing:

Mary had fastened the back buttons of the Little Ones' pinafores together and they were marching about crabwise in little clumps, quite sick with giggles. Valerie had heard that eating paper makes you stammer and was feeding pages to the poodle trying to make him go w-w-woof!

Alison had hidden the budgerigar and put the cat in its cage instead; and Grandmama was having hysterics, seeing him sitting there calmly smiling at her and licking his lips.

Adam had collected the whole of the family mail and posted it in the boiler.

Cecily and William had waxed the seat of the new governess's chair and every time she sat down she shot off again, to her great amazement. And –

Marcus had put a thin layer of paint over her spectacles and the poor thing was seeing everything pink and thought she had conjunctivitis.

All my other children were doing simply dreadful things too.'

'The person you need,' said Great-Aunt Adelaide, 'is Nurse Matilda.'

A funny, funny feeling began to creep over the children, as though, long ago, all this had happened before. They said, quickly: 'Only you can't have her. She's ours.'

And Nurse Matilda stood in the doorway and she smiled – but yet, at the same time two big tears gathered in her eyes and began to roll down her cheeks. And as they rolled – they seemed to roll away with them the last of Nurse Matilda's

wrinkles; and her face wasn't round and brown any more and her nose, like two potatoes, was changing its shape altogether, and even her rusty black dress seemed to be getting all goldeny. And she said: 'Ah, children – you've forgotten how I work! When you do need me, but don't want me – then I must stay. But when you don't need me, and do want me – then I have to go.'

'Oh, no!' cried the children. 'You can't!' And they began to think up naughty things to do immediately. It was strangely difficult, but they did manage to think of a few. 'We still aren't *very* good,' they said hopefully.

'But my children are worse,' pleaded Mrs Green.

'That does seem to be true,' said Nurse Matilda to the children; and she made a bob curtsy to Great-Aunt Adelaide, and said: 'With your permission, then, Ma'am, I shall start work with Mrs Green first thing tomorrow morning.' And she smiled at the children and she looked so lovely – in spite of that one huge sticking-out tooth – that they all started crying and begging, 'Don't go! Don't go!'

But that night, when they were all tucked up in bed, she came round and to every child gave a special kiss and a special hug; and said a rather special 'good night'. And when she had gone out, softly closing the door behind her, they said to each other: 'Did she say "good night"? Wasn't it really "goodbye"?' And they knew in their hearts that it had really been 'goodbye'.

Chapter 8

PERHAPS it was because their hearts were so heavy that night that the children began to dream. At least it was a sort of dream. Afterwards they were never quite sure how much of it had been a dream and how much of it was real – and all the time with that odd feeling that something very much like this had happened before.

The dream was that after Nurse Matilda had closed the doors and all the house was quiet, they got up again and crept out into the garden, and all met together under the willow tree and said: 'Well, we're jolly well not going to stay here without her. Let's go home! Let's run away.'

And all of a sudden, before they knew how it had happened, they *were* running away.

They couldn't stop it.

The house was very quiet, standing tall and gaunt and grim, resentfully watching them go; and it seemed to swing its gate wide open and say, 'All right, go on, get on with it; we don't want you here, anyway.' And they felt themselves almost pushed and hustled out, and when they looked back doubtfully at the gate and wondered whether they shouldn't, after all, go back, it swung-to again and closed itself in their faces; and they saw that there was a sign on it saying, NO RE-ADMITTENS ON ACCOUNT OF INFECTOUIS DISEESE. So anyway, they couldn't go back. They just had to go on.

They began to run. The streets were very dark and quiet, only the gas lamps throwing pools of light, splashed like gold sovereigns along the pavement's edge. The tall houses seemed to close upon them their shuttered eyes, saying disdainfully, 'You are rude and ungrateful, running away from *us*.' 'But we can't help it,' they tried to say. 'We don't really want to, we were only just thinking about it . . .' But their mouths seemed to be full of glue and it only came out M'f, m'f, m'f. And on they ran.

On they ran. Miss Prawn had appeared and

now ran with them, poking them back into line with her parasol while with the other hand she administered great mouthfuls of Evangeline's daily dose. They tried to fob her off with a pink satin handkerchief-sachet, painted with blodgy forget-me-nots, but she only cried out, 'No, no, it'll make me bang into a door-post,' and went on administering the Gregory powders. They had to redouble their speed to get away from her.

They ran and they ran. The Big Ones ran first, the Middlings trailing after them, the Littles trailing after *them*, lugging the Tinies; the Baby last of all, stumping along on its fat bent legs, determined as usual not to be left behind. Sugar and Spice trotted gaily in the rear, full of happy memories, no doubt, of all the nips they had taken at Pug.

On and on. It was rather hard to run and when they looked down they saw that they were wearing Evangeline's button-boots and the boots were filled with Evangeline's dull, red, schoolroom-tea plum jam. And when by much jumping and shaking they managed to dislodge it, the boots were much too large for them and slewed round as they ran, sending them tacking

back and forth across the street, like a fleet of reluctant little ships. And their clothes were Evangeline's hideous dresses, much too small for the Big Ones, much too big for the Littlies; and their hats were Aunt Adelaide's great, overgrown-garden hats, which also were much too big for them and fell down over their eyes and half blinded them. It didn't matter because they just had to keep on running anyway.

And at last – help in sight! Round a corner came cloppeting a four-wheeler cab and a lady and gentleman got out of it and came hastening towards them crying, 'Goot heavints! Vot eest mit ter childrence? You are runnink avay?' 'Oh, Sir Choppup de Lot!' cried the children. 'Oh, Lady de Lot – please help us! We don't *want* to be running away! Please tell us the way back.' But the kindly faces turned towards them and they saw that Sir Choppup and his lady were covered in spots. 'Measles! Chicken-pox! The Plague!' shrieked the children, not able to stop themselves; and their boots took control and sent them tearing off in the opposite direction. Echoes of, 'Med! Ravink! Gone out dere mindts!' came back to them as Sir Choppup handed Lady de Lot back into the cab and turned the horse's head for Dover. 'And all mit little pearts,' said Sir Choppup, sadly. 'Like nanny-koats and pilly-koats, all mit little pearts!'

And it was true: for suddenly their chins had sprouted little golden beards and they bleated as they ran.

They ran and they ran. Between the tall houses, past the Zoo, where all the monkeys came out and pelted them with bits of bun, past Madame Tussaud's, where an Attendant stood, smiling at them helpfully. 'How can we get back to Great-Aunt Adelaide's?' called the children, streeling past him; but he only smiled helpfully on, and they saw that he had eight arms and they were all pointing in different directions.

'Oh,' cried the children, gasping and sobbing, 'if only we could stop!'

But they couldn't. The dawn came, palely creeping up over the roofs of London, glimmering on the tall chimney-pots, rousing the dozy sparrows to a shrill twittering; and they were hungry and thirsty and dreadfully weary, when they turned another corner and there before them was a huge dining-room table piled with things to eat and drink, and behind it was standing Evangeline. 'Oh, Evangeline,' they cried, 'do give us some!'

But Evangeline only broke into jeering laughter and started capering up and down like a gorilla. She was not looking her loveliest, for her podgy round face was coated with porridge and she wore Mademoiselle's red bonnet, its streamers hanging down in front, like an overgrown balcony. But they were not at their best themselves, with their little golden beards, all wearing Evangeline's horrid red and purple dresses and black button-boots. And when, marking time with running steps just to stay where they were, they grabbed at the food, they found that the sausage-rolls were bandages, really, wound up round nothing; and out of each mug of milk hopped a toad, fat and mottled, and hopped on to their heads and sat croaking dismally among the feathers and flowers of Aunt Adelaide's hats. It was joined there by Parrot and Canary – one Parrot and one Canary for each child; and now they must stagger on to a full orchestration of croaks and chirrups and hoarse cries of 'Anchors aweigh!' And so daylight came.

Daylight came, and they were getting to the outskirts of London, running by strange, twisting routes past the Tower – where the ravens formed an escort for them, dismally croaking; past Hampton Court, where they got into the Maze and ran round and round until they were dizzy. Fortunately, the ravens and Parrot and Canary and the toads got dizzy too, and flapped and hopped away; and when they passed Kew Gardens Great-Aunt Adelaide's flowered hats flew off too, to join their relations in the hothouses. If only they could get to the country and find a herd of goats, perhaps they might even get rid of the little beards!

On and on, through the early-morning suburbs, where the housemaids came out on to the steps in their big aprons and starched white caps, to have their jugs filled by the milkman at the door . . . 'Oh, Mr Milkman, please give us some!' cried the children; but when, smiling, he began to pour out the sweet, fresh-smelling milk – alas! there came a hole in the jug and it all ran through. And he looked down into the jug and cried out: 'They've stolen all the milk. Stop thief!'

Stop thief! The children's hearts rose. 'Yes, yes,' they cried, 'stop us, please stop us, don't let us go on running away!' Even the hulks would be better, even deportation would be better than having to run one single solitary step more. 'Stop us, we're thieves, we've stolen Great-Aunt Adelaide's ear trumpet, don't let us get away!'

Along the clean morning pavements, the fine ladies walked with their gentlemen friends, swan-like in their swirly dresses and high, proud hats. 'Stop them!' they cried to the gentlemen, when

they saw the running children. But the gentlemen turned into big umbrellas and ran after the children and whacked them on the backs of their legs with their own much littler umbrellas. 'Faster, faster!' they cried. 'The sun is high in the sky and the road is getting hotter and hotter; if you don't pick up your feet faster, they'll get burnt. It's as hot as a griddle.' 'You know what we can do about *that*,' said the children, beginning to dance. But now they found themselves caught up by the elbows and scurried this way and that by eager hands; like lumps of something horrible, being pushed about by ants. And voices were crying,

'*C'est par ici! Non, non, c'est par là!*' and they saw that the ladies had turned into dozens and dozens of Mademoiselles all chivvying them down the road to the public loo. 'Well, at least when we get there,' thought the children, 'we'll *have* to stop!'

But someone had exchanged the notices, and out of the one marked GENTLEMEN came Miss Prawn, covered in a lather of cheese, and from the one marked LADIES appeared Professor Schnorr, clad only in his trousers, with his big black beard spread out over his front. But what looked like his tummy was a large, pink sofa cushion, really, and when he saw Miss Prawn, her pale shrimp-pink form glimmering through the decent lather, he flung it from him and bolted off round the corner. The cushion burst and all the feathers flew up in a cloud and settled softly upon lathered Miss Prawn. Like a huge baby gosling covered in down, she flew up urgently cackling into the air; landed again, took one look at the children's legs and with outstretched beak, gave chase.

On and on and on. The last of the houses came and they were out in the country, pounding along the empty lanes between the tall hedges, where the milkwort and ragged robin made all the air sweet with the scent of green juices. They saw Cook and Gumble and Fiddle, carrying trays, but the moment they set eyes on the children they took to their heels and with great kangaroo-hops leapt and lolloped away; and they had been running since bed-time last night – and now it was afternoon.

And suddenly – bowling ahead of them in an open carriage – Mr and Mrs Haversack, with Adolphus sitting squashed in between them. 'Oh, Adolphus, oh, Mr Haversack, oh, Mrs Haversack!' cried the children, catching up with them, jog-trotting along beside the carriage, 'do let us get in with you, do give us a lift, we're so hot and tired and we can't stop running away . . .'

Mrs Haversack bowed to right and left. 'Poor things! What can we do for them, Haversack? Advise me!'

But Mr Haversack only fluffed up his long golden beard and said 'Prrrrrr-up!' and all of a sudden Adolphus was growing strangely black and shiny in the face and his nose was growing longer and stiff whiskers were growing out on either side of it. 'A dolphin! He's turned into a

dolphin!' cried Mrs Haversack, and prodded the coachman in the back with her parasol. 'Quick – to the Zoo!' The children heard his honk-honk-honking as the carriage bowled away.

The long day passed – the long, long, weary day. Evening came. They breasted a hill and came upon a herd of goats, sitting by the roadside, scratching at their flanks with their little black hooves. 'Where are you going?' bleated the goats. 'And why have you got our beards?' 'Line up across the road,' cried the children, 'and stop us running away, and we'll give them back to you.' For they saw now that the goats had indeed no hair upon their chinny-chin-chins.

So the goats lined up across the road and the children stopped (jerking down up and down, marking time, but at least not actually running) and tugged at the beards. And the goats stopped scratching and poked forward their naked chins. And in a little while . . .

In a little while all the goats were bearded, but not scratching any longer with their little polished hooves; and the children had no beards, but scratched as they ran.

Darkness fell and the stars came out and twinkled down upon them; and they ran and they ran and they ran. And someone had cut the elastic of their knickers and the starched, frilly legs had fallen down round their ankles and impeded their every step. 'We know now,' they said, sobbing, to one another, 'how the Baby feels with its nappies always coming down.' And they passed it back, down the long crocodile of stumbling children, the mumbling, grumbling, tumbling children, staggering on, falling, scrambling up again, tripping and regaining their feet once more – 'Poor Baby, now we know how you feel . . .!'

And an idea began to grow. It grew and it grew; starting with the Big Ones, making its way back to the Middling Ones, through the Little Ones, back to the Littlest Ones, right down to the Baby itself, forging along, its fat little elbows going like pistons, on its two little fat, bent legs . . . And when the idea came to the Baby it stopped running, absolutely stopped running, in that one moment; and sat down in a round, mournful bundle in the middle of the road and put its round pudding fists in its eyes and sobbed out: 'Wonk Nurk Magiggy! Wairg my Nurk Magiggy?'

And a voice said out of the darkness, and as

velvet as the darkness: 'Darling Baby – I am here.'

And there she was – a warmth, a glow, a golden radiance in the chill and darkness of the night: Nurse Matilda.

And she gave one thump with her stick: and all the children stopped running, and cried out: 'Oh, Nurse Matilda – why didn't we think of you before? Please take us home.'

And Nurse Matilda stood there and smiled at them; and she said, 'Oh, my wicked ones, my naughty, naughty children! – just give me one good reason why I should!'

The children didn't stop to think. They said: 'We were only running away because we didn't want to stay without *you.*'

And Nurse Matilda smiled and smiled; and when she smiled, it seemed to the children that really she must be the loveliest person in all the world. Except . . . Well, really you had to say it: Except for that terrible Tooth.

And at that moment while they were thinking it – couldn't help thinking it – what do you think happened? That Tooth of hers flew out and landed in the middle of the road at the children's feet.

And it began to grow.

It grew and it grew. It grew until it was the size of a matchbox. It grew until it was the size of a snuff-box. It grew until it was the size of a shoe-box – of a tuck-box – of a suitcase – of a packing-case – of a trunk: of a big trunk, a huge trunk, a simply enormous trunk. And all the while as it grew, it was taking shape – growing golden and shining and beautifully curved, growing windows on either side of it, in curly golden frames; growing hollow inside with a soft leather lining: growing big golden wheels: growing a coachman sitting up on the box above it, growing a footman in frogged coat and plush breeches, standing holding the door: growing a team of six beautiful horses, tossing their proud heads, stamping their shining hooves, jingling their harness, eager to be off. And into the coach climbed Nurse Matilda, carrying the sleepy Baby in her arms; and after her climbed the children, one after the other, pushing in, piling in and yet seeming each to find a comfortable place with lots of room; all clustered round Nurse Matilda as she sat in the centre of the soft, leather-backed seat; curled up around her, sleepily, safely, like

drowsy bees round a golden honey-pot. And clip clop, clip clop, went the shining hooves, and nid-nod, nid-nod, went the droopy heads . . . And there came a big gate – but it wasn't Great-Aunt Adelaide's gate; and there was a curving drive up to a big front door, standing wide open; and shining down at them were the friendly, welcoming, lighted windows – of their own dear home!

And – how could it have happened that, to each child, it seemed as if loving arms came around him and he was lifted up gently and his weary head cradled against a kind shoulder? And he was carried softly and silently into the house and up the wide stairs and slipped into his own warm cosy bed: washed and brushed and changed into night clothes, teeth cleaned, prayers said and peacefully dreaming . . . Dreaming that he was running away: but would wake up in his own bed in the morning, all safe and sound – only quite, quite certain never to run away again.

When they did wake up next morning – Nurse Matilda was gone.